MARY-KATE & ASHLEY

Starring in

SCHOOL DANCE PARTY ™

A novelization by Eliza Willard

Based on the teleplay by
Neil Steinberg

■HarperEntertainment
An Imprint of HarperCollins*Publishers*

A PARACHUTE PRESS BOOK

PARACHUTE
PRESS

Parachute Publishing, L.L.C.
156 Fifth Avenue
New York, NY 10010

DUALSTAR
PUBLICATIONS

Dualstar Publications
c/o Thorne and Company
1801 Century Park East
Los Angeles, CA 90067

HarperEntertainment

An Imprint of HarperCollins*Publishers*
10 East 53rd Street, New York, NY 10022

Book created and produced by Parachute Publishing, L.L.C., in cooperation with
Dualstar Publications, a division of Dualstar Entertainment Group, Inc., published by
HarperEntertainment, an imprint of HarperCollins Publishers.

For information address HarperCollins Publishers Inc.,
10 East 53rd Street, New York, NY 10022.

ISBN 0-06-106667-2

HarperCollins®, ■®, and HarperEntertainment™ are trademarks of
HarperCollins Publishers Inc.

First printing: September 2001

Printed in the United States of America

mary-kateandashley.com
America Online Keyword: mary-kateandashley

Visit HarperEntertainment on the World Wide Web at
www.harpercollins.com

10 9 8 7 6 5 4 3 2 1

CHAPTER ONE

"Another Monday, another week of school...." Ashley said cheerfully as she and her sister, Mary-Kate, climbed the steps to Fleming High School.

"Yup." Mary-Kate pushed her shiny blond hair behind her shoulders and grinned at Ashley. "Hanging in the halls...the cafeteria..."

"Not to mention a few classes in between," Ashley added, pulling open the front door to the school.

She and her sister stepped inside. The halls were bustling with kids talking and laughing.

"Hey, there's Hannah!" Ashley waved to a petite girl with long, thick, dark hair and big brown eyes, and headed over to her. Hannah Holmes was Ashley's closest friend—after Mary-Kate, of course.

"Morning," Hannah said. She slammed her locker shut and followed Mary-Kate and Ashley down the hall to their lockers. "Love the skirt, Ashley."

Ashley was wearing a red-and-blue patchwork miniskirt with a white T-shirt. Mary-Kate wore jeans that she'd decorated herself with fabric patches on the pockets and beads along the cuffs.

"Thanks," Ashley said. "My mom made it out of an old blanket that Piglet clawed up." Piglet was the girls' cat.

Ashley twirled the combination to her locker. Mary-Kate opened her locker, too, and picked out some notebooks for class. Then she stopped. She seemed to be listening to something.

"Hear that?" she asked Ashley and Hannah.

"I don't hear anything," Ashley said. "Other than the usual before-school traffic."

"Something's going on," Mary-Kate said slowly. She was still listening to the buzz of the crowd in the hallway.

"Any good gossip?" Ashley asked.

"Maybe...." Mary-Kate said, concentrating harder. Then she shook her head. "Nope. I think some major event is coming up."

"Hey, guys!" Betsy Browner rushed up to the three girls. "Have you heard?"

"What?" Mary-Kate, Ashley, and Hannah all asked at once.

"The fall dance!" Betsy gushed. "It's coming up in just three weeks. We're calling it Cyberdance!"

Hannah's mouth fell open. She stared at Mary-Kate. "How did you do that?" she asked. "How did you know there was big news?"

Mary-Kate grinned and shrugged.

Ashley smiled at her sister. "She has a gift."

"What are you guys talking about?" Betsy demanded. She was a tall girl with glossy black hair. "Didn't you hear what I just said?"

Mary-Kate didn't answer Betsy right away. Then Betsy's news must have sunk in, because Mary-Kate suddenly jumped up and squealed. "A fall dance!" she cried. "That's so awesome!"

"As chairperson of the social committee," Betsy said, "I'm organizing a subcommittee to plan the dance. Any volunteers?"

"I'll be on the dance committee," Mary-Kate said eagerly. "I've got tons of ideas."

"Good," Betsy said. "We'll meet after school in the student lounge." She hurried off to tell more people the exciting news.

"I can't wait!" Hannah said. "Who are you going to the dance with, Mary-Kate?"

"I don't know," Mary-Kate said. "But whoever it is, I hope he's a good dancer. I'd hate to be embarrassed on the dance floor."

"Hey, what's going on ladies?" Ashley's new boyfriend, Rick Morgan, walked up and rested his hand on Ashley's shoulder. Rick and Ashley had started dating each other two weeks ago.

Ashley turned and smiled at him. *He's so cute,* she thought, gazing up at his dark blue eyes, wavy brown hair, and warm smile. *Sometimes I have to pinch myself to really believe we're together.* "Betsy just told us we're having a dance," she explained. "Cyberdance. I guess it's a computer theme."

"Excellent," Rick said. He playfully poked Ashley in the ribs. "And who are *you* going with?"

"Oh, I don't know," Ashley teased. "Some geek, probably."

"Well, don't make any plans," Rick said. "Because I know one geek who really wants to take you to that dance."

Ashley felt her cheeks grow warm. She knew Rick was talking about himself—even though he wasn't a geek at all.

A tall, blond, athletic-looking girl walked past. Ashley froze. It was Kelly Benton, Rick's old girlfriend. They'd only broken up about a month before. Ashley didn't know why they'd broken up. But she had a feeling that Kelly wanted Rick back.

"Hi, Rick," Kelly said. She gave him a little wave.

Ashley and Hannah exchanged glances. They'd both noticed that Kelly had said hello only to Rick—and not to the girls.

4

"Hey, Kelly," Rick said politely. He didn't look at her as she walked away.

That made Ashley feel a little better. Maybe he didn't like Kelly anymore.

The bell rang. "I've got to run," Rick said. "See you later Ashley, okay?"

Ashley nodded and watched her boyfriend bound down the hall. He turned and waved to her right before he entered a classroom.

"I know *one* person who's got a date for the dance all set up," Mary-Kate whispered into her ear.

"Yeah," Ashley said, smiling. "Me, too."

"Hey!" Betsy shouted. "HEY!" She stood in front of the blackboard in the student lounge, waving her arms. The school day was over, and fifteen students had volunteered for the fall dance committee.

But Mary-Kate and the rest of the committee were busy talking, laughing, and lounging on the sofas. Nobody was listening to Betsy.

"Hey!" Betsy screeched again. "MY DAD KNOWS *NSYNC!"

The room suddenly hushed. Betsy grinned triumphantly and said, "Now that I have your attention, can we please start the meeting?"

Mary-Kate leaned back in her seat. Everybody

knew that Betsy's father was a big record producer. She was always bragging about all the stars he brought over to their house for dinner.

"As you all know, the dance is called Cyberdance," Betsy said. "The theme is the Internet. I thought we could decorate the gym to look like cyberspace." She paused. "The only problem is, I have no idea what cyberspace looks like."

"Maybe we could make it look kind of like the inside of a computer," Dan Owens suggested. "You know, use colored wires instead of streamers, and weird blinking lights to look like microchips."

"We can send out invitations to the dance by E-mail," Marie Duncan added.

"Those are great ideas," Betsy said, jotting them down on a piece of paper. "I also thought the dance could have a king and a queen—the way we do at prom. The King and Queen of Cyberspace."

"Yeah!" Darcy Mason agreed. "Why don't we set up a Cyberdance website? We can have photos and info about all the candidates for King and Queen of Cyberspace—and kids can vote for their favorites on-line!"

"Perfect," Betsy said. "One of us will tally the votes at the dance, and we'll crown the King and Queen right there."

The room began to buzz with excitement. *This dance is really going to be fun,* Mary-Kate thought. *But I know how it can be even more fun.*

"I have an idea," Mary-Kate said. "We could get a singing group together. You know, a boy band like the Backstreet Boys or *NSYNC. The group can sing at the dance and serenade the King and Queen of Cyberspace when we crown them."

The buzz in the room grew even louder. Marie Duncan nudged Mary-Kate. "Great idea!" she said.

"So where will this group come from?" Betsy asked. "We don't have any bands like that here at school—unless you count the chorus."

"They can be from our own class," Mary-Kate said. "We'll audition some boys and choose the five best singers. Maybe Mr. Moreland can teach them a few songs."

Mr. Moreland was the Fleming High music teacher. He was young and pretty cool.

The four boys on the dance committee stared at Mary-Kate as if she were crazy, but the girls loved the idea.

"Mary-Kate, I'll put you in charge of the auditions," Betsy said.

"Can I help?" Darcy asked.

"Me, too!" Marie said.

"That's up to Mary-Kate," Betsy said. "But we do need people to be in charge of other things—like decorations and refreshments. I'll post a list and you can all sign up for stuff...." She paused. All the girls had surrounded Mary-Kate and were chattering about how they could audition the boys. They had stopped listening to Betsy again.

"HEY!" Betsy boomed. "I HAD LUNCH WITH BRITNEY SPEARS!"

The group quieted down. Mary-Kate rolled her eyes.

"I have another announcement to make," Betsy said. "The DJ at the dance will be a special surprise guest." Betsy paused for dramatic effect. Then she smiled as if she had a really juicy secret.

Wow, Mary-Kate thought. *This is going to be huge.*

"Who? Who?" everyone wanted to know.

"I can't tell you now," Betsy said. "No one will know until the night of the dance."

The student lounge erupted in a roar of chatter.

Mary-Kate could hardly stand the suspense. With Betsy's father's connections, the special DJ might be a real celebrity. Maybe even a superstar!

CHAPTER TWO

"Maybe the special-guest DJ will be Madonna!" Ashley whispered Tuesday morning. She was sitting in science class with Mary-Kate and Hannah. Mary-Kate had told her about Betsy's announcement the night before. They had been trying to guess who it could be ever since.

"Come on," Hannah whispered back. "Madonna? At Fleming? Spinning records at a dance? That'll never happen."

"It's got to be somebody cool," Mary-Kate said. "Remember that time Betsy's dad brought Mark West to one of our basketball games?"

"Who could forget?" Ashley replied. Mark West was one of her sister's favorite rock stars. He'd accidentally brushed Mary-Kate's hand at the game, and Mary-Kate refused to wash it for a whole week.

"I hope you're discussing acids and bases over there, girls," Ms. Denby, the science teacher, said. Ashley, Mary-Kate, and Hannah immediately stopped talking. "We're going to do a lab experi-

9

ment now," Ms. Denby went on. "Everybody pick a partner."

Ashley glanced at Hannah. "Be my partner?"

Hannah nodded.

Jesse Bates tapped Mary-Kate on her shoulder. "Got a partner yet, MK?" He and Mary-Kate had been friends since kindergarten. He always called her MK.

"Guess I do now." Mary-Kate grinned and they headed for a lab station.

Hannah and Ashley took the station next to theirs. Ashley watched Mary-Kate and Jesse out of the corner of her eye. Jesse was really smart, Ashley thought, and kind of cute, too. He was small and wiry with brown hair and long-lashed blue eyes. And anyone could see how much he liked Mary-Kate. Ashley knew her sister liked Jesse a lot, too, but she was always making fun of how dorky and klutzy he could be.

"Hey, MK—watch this." Jesse held up a beaker. "If I take calcium carbonate and weak hydrochloric acid..." He added the two chemicals to the beaker. Then he took a small stick and lit it in the Bunsen burner. "Add a small flame and—you get beaker bark."

"Huh?" Mary-Kate said. "What's beaker bark?"

"You'll see." Jesse held the flame to the beaker.

Arf! A funny barking sound came out of the beaker. Mary-Kate laughed. Jesse did it again and Mary-Kate laughed harder.

He's trying to impress her, Ashley thought as she watched them. *But I'm not sure chemistry is the way to Mary-Kate's heart.*

"I think Jesse likes you," Ashley told her sister in the hallway after class. "Maybe he'll ask you to the dance."

"Jesse? We're just friends." Mary-Kate shrugged. "And anyway, he's such a klutz. Not my type at—" She stopped.

Ashley followed her sister's gaze down the hall. Alex Marks was headed in their direction. Alex was tall and broad-shouldered with dark blond hair that fell across one eye. He was the star of the soccer team. He landed the lead in almost every school play, too.

Mary-Kate leaned close to her sister. "Now, *that's* my type," she whispered. "Too bad he'll probably never notice me...." She heaved a big sigh.

The girls stopped talking as Alex passed them. He glanced at Mary-Kate and shot her a big smile.

Mary-Kate gasped. "Did you see that?" she asked Ashley.

Ashley's eyes were wide. "Wow. What was that about?"

"I don't know," Mary-Kate said. "He's never even *looked* at me before!" She paused to stare down the hall as Alex turned a corner and disappeared. "Do you think—"

"What?" Ashley asked. "Do I think what?"

Mary-Kate struggled to get the words out. "Do you think...Alex...maybe—"

Ashley threw up her hands. "Spit it out!"

"Do you think he...he could like me?" Mary-Kate finally sputtered. "Is it possible he might even..."

Ashley knew it was too much for her sister to say aloud. "Ask you to the dance?" she finished for her. "Why not?"

"Amazing." Mary-Kate leaned against a row of lockers and sighed again. Then she looked at Ashley very seriously. "Do you think he's a good dancer?"

"Hey, Mary-Kate," a voice said.

Mary-Kate was in the library, studying for the Spanish test coming up next period. She glanced up to see David Jorgensen smiling down at her.

"Want a hint for the Spanish test?" he asked. "Remember this sentence—*Tu eres muy bonita.*" He grinned at her and went over to sit at a carrel.

Mary-Kate flipped through her Spanish diction-ary. *"Bonita, bonita...* Why can't I remember what that means?" she said to herself. Then she found it. "'*Bonita*—pretty.'"

She glanced across the room at David. He was watching her. He smiled and gave her a little wave.

"Whoa." Now David Jorgensen was flirting with her? Mary-Kate had known him since third grade. All he'd ever done was knock her down when they played kickball.

She touched a strand of her hair. *Could it be that new shampoo?* she wondered. *Maybe it has some kind of special ingredient in it....*

"Hey, Mary-Kate." Jake O'Harrow sat down at her table. "What's up?"

"Just studying for a Spanish test," Mary-Kate replied. She glanced at him from across the table. *What does he want?* she wondered. Jake played guitar and had his own band. He usually acted as if he were already a rock star. Too cool for school— and for Mary-Kate's crowd.

"Oh," Jake said. "Well, good luck." He smiled at her.

Mary-Kate half-smiled back and tried to hit the books again. But she kept feeling Jake's eyes boring into her head. She looked up again. He was still sitting there, grinning.

"Um, what?" Mary-Kate asked him.

"Nothing, nothing at all. I'm just sitting here. You know, sitting in the library. At school and everything."

"O-*kay*." Mary-Kate tried to study again, but she couldn't concentrate with Jake staring at her.

"*Hola!*" Kevin Bly pulled up a chair beside her. "I've got the Spanish test nailed. Want some help?" He reached over and touched her forearm.

Mary-Kate stared at Kevin's hand on her arm, then at his face. *Has he lost his mind?* she wondered. *Why would I want Kevin's help in Spanish? He's getting a D!*

"Like, on the vocabulary part?" Kevin said. "I've got it all figured out. If you're talking about a chick, you put an *a* on the end of the word. And if you're talking about a dude, you put an *o*. Like, you say, 'That chick is really fine-a.' Or, 'Man, that dude is so cool-o.' Or is it coolio?"

Mary-Kate raised an eyebrow. "Thanks, but I think I can manage on my own. Really."

"Leave her alone, Kevin," Jake said. "Can't you see she's trying to concentrate?"

"I'm just trying to help out a fellow student," Kevin replied.

Mary-Kate closed her book and stood up. "I think I'll go sit at a carrel." She gathered her things and started toward the carrels, but stopped when David Jorgensen waved to her again. "On second thought," she said, "maybe I've studied enough."

Mary-Kate walked out of the library. As she pulled open the door, all three guys called out, "Bye, Mary-Kate!"

The librarian shushed them.

Wow, Mary-Kate thought. *What's going on? Am I suddenly the hottest babe in school or what?*

Mary-Kate didn't have time to try to figure out her instant popularity. After Spanish she went straight to the main bulletin board to hang a poster announcing auditions for the boy band.

I've got to come up with a good name for the band, she thought as she pressed tacks into the corkboard. Betsy had already hung up a poster announcing the dance and the contest for King and Queen of Cyberspace.

A chunky boy with curly brown hair stopped to read the poster. "Hi, Mary-Kate," he said.

Mary-Kate fastened the last tack and turned to look at him. She'd seen the boy around, but she didn't know his name. He smiled at her. "Uh, hi," she said.

They stood there awkwardly for a minute. Mary-

Kate waited for him to say something else or go on his way. But he just kept smiling at her.

This is really weird, Mary-Kate thought. She didn't know what to do.

Finally the boy said, "Well…bye." But he didn't move. He still stood in front of her, grinning like crazy.

Mary-Kate glanced at the boy, then back at the poster she was hanging. The band, she realized. Could that be why she was attracting so much attention?

"Bye," Mary-Kate told the boy quickly. *This is my chance to escape,* she thought. She hurried away down the hall toward the cafeteria for lunch.

Once safely there, she passed through the lunch line, picking up a turkey sandwich and a fruit salad. Then she spotted Ashley and Hannah at a table in the corner and went to join them.

"You'll never believe what just happened," Mary-Kate began. But Ashley didn't even look up. She was sitting with her chin in her hands, frowning. "What's the matter?" Mary-Kate asked her.

"Everything!" Ashley replied. "The dance is already ruined!"

CHAPTER THREE

"What are you talking about?" Mary-Kate asked. "What do you mean, the dance is ruined?"

Ashley sighed. She didn't really want to talk about it, but her sister was staring at her. So was Hannah.

"It's Rick," she said, picking up her fork. She started poking at her plate of chicken. "You know how he's so into computers. He walks around with his Palm Pilot all the time, checking his E-mail...."

So?" Hannah asked, frowning.

"So he's going to run for King of Cyberspace!" Ashley cried.

"That's great," Mary-Kate said. "Everybody likes Rick. He'll win for sure."

"I know. That's the trouble," Ashley said. "Don't you see? He'll win—and some other girl will be Queen. They'll have to dance together in front of everybody. And they'll be like a *couple*!"

"It won't mean anything," Hannah pointed out. "Rick will still be your date."

"But it *will* mean something," Ashley insisted. "Because Kelly Benton is running for Queen!"

Ashley couldn't stop thinking that Kelly Benton was trying to get Rick back. She always seemed to be around. And Kelly was the kind of girl who'd do anything to get what she wanted.

"So what?" Mary-Kate said. "Rick is nuts about you! Anyway, you've got nothing to worry about. The answer to your problem is simple."

"What?" Ashley threw her sister a suspicious glance. Mary-Kate was always saying things were simple, but they hardly ever turned out that way.

"All you have to do is run for Queen yourself," Mary-Kate replied. "I'll nominate you. You know lots of people. I bet if you campaign hard enough, you could win! Then it will be *you* up there dancing with Rick—the King and Queen of Cyberspace!"

"Brilliant!" Hannah cried.

"I don't know." Ashley hesitated. "What if I *don't* win? Then it will be even worse."

"Come on, Ashley," Hannah replied. "How could you *not* win with us on your team?" She squinted at her. "The first thing you need is a new wardrobe. We'll all go to the mall this afternoon and find the perfect Cyber Queen clothes."

Ashley brightened up a little. Mary-Kate and

18

Hannah seemed so sure of themselves. *They really think I have a chance,* Ashley thought. *Maybe I do.*

"Okay. I'm in," she told them. "I'll run for Queen. Anything that involves shopping can't be bad, right?"

"Come on, girl—let's get glam!" Hannah said in the mall after school. She grabbed Ashley's arm.

Ashley found herself being tugged toward Electromagnetic, the hottest clothes store in the mall.

"I'll meet you guys back here later, okay?" Mary-Kate said. "I've got to get some sheet music and karaoke CDs."

"Right *now?*" Hannah asked.

"I'm starting the auditions for the singing group tomorrow," Mary-Kate explained. "Do you think any boys will show up?"

Hannah shrugged. "Probably. Be sure to pick out the hottest ones, okay?"

Mary-Kate laughed. "No problem. I'll be over at Sing-Sing."

"See you," Ashley called as Hannah dragged her inside Electromagnetic.

Hannah pointed to a rack of shimmering, sequined tops. "Let's look at those," she said.

But something else caught Ashley's eye. Actually, some*one.* A tall, leggy blond girl stood at the counter, trying on tiaras. She had her back to them.

It can't be, Ashley thought as she stared at the girl. *Please don't let it be her.*

The girl turned around to study herself in a mirror. Ashley's heart sank. It *was* her—Kelly Benton.

Kelly spotted Ashley and waved. "Hi, girls," she said. "Don't I look great in a tiara? I bet I'll look even better in one made for a cyberqueen."

Kelly is way more popular than I am, Ashley thought. *How can I ever compete with her?*

"I heard Rick is running for King of Cyberspace," Kelly said with a sly, confident smile. "He's so cool. He's always liked cool girls, too."

"Ashley's cool," Hannah said.

Kelly laughed. "Whatever you say, Hannah." She stared at Ashley. "You really don't seem like Rick's type, Audrey."

"That's *Ashley*," Ashley replied through gritted teeth. She was fuming. *Rick doesn't care about who's cool and who's not,* she wanted to say. But then she thought, *Maybe he does.* She couldn't help noticing how gracefully Kelly moved. Everything she wore was the latest style and looked just perfect on her.

Ashley couldn't help thinking Kelly was cooler than she was, but she'd never realized that Rick cared about that kind of stuff so much. *Then again, he used to go out with Kelly, right?*

"You won't be laughing so hard when Ashley is crowned Queen of Cyberspace," Hannah said.

Ashley elbowed Hannah in the ribs. She wished Hannah hadn't said that. Now it was too late to back out.

"Oh, are you running, too?" Kelly asked with a fake smile. "That's sweet. Good luck."

"Thanks," Ashley said, trying to be gracious. "Good luck to you, too." She grabbed Hannah by the arm and tugged her toward the sequined tops.

"I can't believe that girl," Hannah whispered as they huddled near the dressing rooms. "It's so obvious she thinks she can get Rick back. She doesn't even try to hide it!"

"Maybe she's right," Ashley said quietly. "Maybe she *can* get him back."

"What?" Hannah cried. "That's ridiculous. You and Rick are perfect together, and you know it."

"Yeah," Ashley mumbled. But she wondered if that was really true. She didn't want to lose her boyfriend to Kelly. Being crowned Queen of Cyberspace was becoming more important by the second.

"I know I can be just as hip as Kelly," Ashley said, eyeing a pair of leopard-print pants. "I just haven't tried hard enough." She turned to Hannah and added, "But I have no idea where to start."

Hannah glanced at Kelly, who was sashaying out of the store. "Well, what makes Kelly so cool?" She thought for a minute. "She's totally athletic. She's broken every track record in school. She always wears the latest clothes—"

"She always acts as if she's above everyone and everything," Ashley said. "Like she's too cool to let stuff get to her."

"Yeah," Hannah agreed. "And everybody thinks it's true." She paused. "My mother always says, 'If you act like a queen, you'll *be* a queen.'"

"Hmmm." Ashley thought about that. *Kelly definitely doesn't make friends by being nice to people,* she told herself. *Yet she's totally popular. It must be because she's such a superstar jock. Everybody loves a winner.*

"Can I help you two?" A skinny salesgirl smiled at them. Her short dark hair was tied in tiny knots all over her head and clipped with baby barrettes.

"My friend needs some new clothes," Hannah spoke up. "The hottest clothes you've got."

"I know just what you're looking for," the salesgirl said. She dug through a rack and pulled out a metallic miniskirt as shiny as a mirror. It glared so much that Ashley had to turn her eyes away.

"This looks great with robot boots." The salesgirl pointed to a pair of hot-pink, ribbed boots.

Ashley thought they looked like a set of pink tires stacked on top of one another. "Those look a little weird to me," she said slowly.

"Honey, they're all the rage in New York," the salesgirl insisted. "Trust me."

Ashley glanced at Hannah. "Let's go to the Sports Connection," she whispered. "I think they'll have what I need."

She grabbed Hannah by the wrist and pulled her out of the boutique. They hurried to the Sports Connection on the other side of the mall.

"Ashley, what are we doing here?" Hannah asked. "You're not into sports."

"Well, I will be now," Ashley said. "Everybody knows who Kelly is because she's a track star, right? And people will vote for her because of it, too."

"Maybe," Hannah admitted. "But I don't get—"

"I can be a jock, too," Ashley said. "How hard could it be? It's just running—and the right athletic gear."

She quickly combed through racks of track suits, sneakers, and workout clothes, picking out the brightest-colored, coolest-looking stuff.

I'll just have to beat Kelly at her own game, Ashley thought. *I've got to make everybody vote for me!*

CHAPTER FOUR

"This is it," Ashley said as she hopped out of bed the next morning. "Day One of the new me."

She stood in front of her closet, staring at all the clothes she'd bought at the mall yesterday. "Let's see...I think I'll be a tennis player today." She picked out a black-and-white tank top and a short white tennis skirt with white socks and white tennis shoes. Then she looked in the mirror.

"All I need is a racket," she said, satisfied. "And the ability to play tennis...."

"Ashley!" Mary-Kate called to her from downstairs. "Are you ready yet? I'm leaving!"

"One second!" Ashley shouted back.

She quickly braided her blond hair, then grabbed her backpack. She was ready to roll.

Ashley caught up with Mary-Kate as her sister was walking out the front door. Mary-Kate gasped when she saw her.

"What have you done with Ashley?" Mary-Kate demanded.

"Very funny," Ashley snapped.

"No, really." Mary-Kate couldn't stop gawking. "Is there some kind of costume party today? Why are you wearing a tennis outfit?"

"I'm a jock," Ashley said. "Didn't you know?"

Mary-Kate raised an eyebrow. "No, I sure didn't know. I've seen you with a tennis racket. You hit everything but the ball."

"I never said I was actually going to *play* tennis," Ashley said. "All I have to do is *look* as if I can play tennis."

About twenty minutes later Ashley was strolling through the school halls to her locker. She noticed the other kids staring at her and whispering.

Ashley smiled to herself. *It's working!* she thought. *This superjock gear really gets people's attention. From now on, this is the new me.*

"Hey, Ashley." She turned to see Rick standing behind her. He stared at her as she spun around, showing off her new clothes.

"What's with the outfit?" he asked. "I've never seen you look so...so..."

"Athletic?" Ashley finished for him. "Oh, I *love* sports. You probably never knew that about me."

"No, I didn't," Rick said, shrugging. "But that's cool."

I knew it! Ashley thought. *I knew he liked sporty*

girls. "I've decided to run for Queen of Cyberspace, by the way," she announced.

Rick smiled. "Great. I hope you win."

"Thanks," Ashley said. She felt like throwing her arms around him and giving him a hug. *I'd better not,* she decided. *Got to play it cool. Like Kelly would.*

Rick's cell phone started ringing.

"Well," Ashley said. "Gotta fly. See you." She hurried away. When she glanced back, Rick was staring after her with a funny look on his face.

At the end of the day Mary-Kate grabbed her boom box and a pile of CDs and headed for the auditorium. Several girls had volunteered to help her with the auditions. But when the time came, they were all busy with other after-school projects.

I wonder if any boys will show up, Mary-Kate thought. *Most of the guys I know are so shy. I can't imagine them singing in front of people.*

She crossed the courtyard and went into the auditorium building. To her surprise, the hall outside the auditorium was crowded with boys. Mary-Kate stopped and stared at them.

They can't all be here for the auditions, she said to herself. *Can they?*

She fought her way through the mob and

26

opened the auditorium door. Then she stopped again, stunned.

The room was filled with boys—dozens and dozens of them!

"What's going on?" Mary-Kate asked.

"We're here for the tryouts," one boy told her. "Are you Mary-Kate?"

She nodded and gulped. She had never imagined so many of them would want to sing at a dance!

She marched up to the front of the room and stood on the stage. "Hi, guys," she said. "Welcome. Are you sure you're all in the right place? I'm auditioning people to sing at the fall dance."

A murmur went through the room. Nobody left.

"I—I guess I'm kind of surprised there are so many of you," Mary-Kate said. "I mean, it's not *that* big a deal."

Someone laughed. "Yeah, right. No big deal at all!"

The crowd erupted in nervous laughter. Mary-Kate was baffled.

"Um, o-*kay*," she said, glancing around the room in confusion.

"You mean you don't know?" one boy called out.

Mary-Kate frowned. *Know what?*

CHAPTER FIVE

"Give us a break, Mary-Kate," Jake O'Harrow said. "It's all over school. Betsy Browner is arranging a special guest DJ for the dance, right?"

"Well, yes," Mary-Kate said. "But—"

"It's going to be a record producer," Jake interrupted. "That's what everyone's saying, anyway."

"And he's looking for a hot new band to promote," Kevin Bly put in.

"The guys in this group are going to be rich and famous!" Jake said.

The boys rushed the stage. "I'm going first!" one cried.

"No—me first!" another shouted.

Mary-Kate sat down on the stage and covered her head. *What have I gotten myself into? And where are all those girls who said they'd help me?* she wondered.

She jumped to her feet. "All right!" She clapped her hands for attention. "Everybody sit down!"

The boys scrambled to find seats. "The name of

the group will be the Cyberpunks," she announced. "And we're going to choose five guys for the group. I'll audition you in order of your seats, starting here." She pointed to the first row. "You can go first," she told the boy.

A door opened at the back of the auditorium and Ashley slipped inside. She walked coolly down the center aisle and up to where Mary-Kate stood on the stage.

"Ashley—what are you doing here?" Mary-Kate asked.

"I thought I'd help you with the auditions," Ashley said. "Is that all right?"

"Sure," Mary-Kate said, feeling a little relieved. "I could definitely use some help. We're just getting started."

She and Ashley sat on the edge of the stage. Mary-Kate pulled a clipboard out of her backpack and scribbled David Jorgensen's name on it. David stood center stage, clearing his throat.

"What's got you so interested in the band all of a sudden?" Mary-Kate whispered to her sister.

"I heard about the record producer," Ashley whispered back. "So I figured that a lot of boys would want to try out. And if I'm here, they'll get to know me. It might bring me a lot of votes."

Mary-Kate rolled her eyes. Ashley was getting so caught up in this Queen of Cyberspace thing. And it was only the first day of her campaign!

"Okay, David," Mary-Kate said. "We're ready."

David put a karaoke CD into the boom box and pressed Play. He began to sing along in a high-pitched, off-tune voice. "Tell me, babe...Do I have to go?..." He spun around on his heel, tripped, and fell flat on his back.

Ashley squeezed her lips together, trying not to laugh.

"Thank you, David," Mary-Kate said politely. "Next!"

"He doesn't really strike me as boy-band material," Ashley whispered.

Mary-Kate gave her a glance that said, "Shhh!"

Joseph Serio, a tall, thin boy with a long, serious face, mounted the stage next. "I've been studying voice since I was three," he announced.

"Great," Mary-Kate said. "Let's hear it." *It can't be any worse than David,* she thought. "Which CD do you want to use?"

"Oh, I don't need accompaniment," Joseph said. He stood up straighter, opened his mouth, and began to sing an aria from an opera. *"O sole mio..."*

Ashley didn't say a word. She just glanced at

Mary-Kate, who sighed. The boys in the auditorium shifted restlessly in their seats. "Next!" Mary-Kate called.

Her heartbeat speeded up when Alex Marks took the stage. He looked calm and confident. *He's so cute*, Mary-Kate thought for the millionth time.

"I brought my own CD," he announced. He popped it into the player and began to sing an old Jackson 5 song. He moved easily across the stage as he sang.

Mary-Kate melted. "He's perfect," she whispered.

"I'll say," Ashley agreed. "The guy can really sing. Too bad he's so stuck-up."

Mary-Kate glared at her sister. A few minutes later Alex finished. A bunch of guys clapped. "Thank you, Alex," Mary-Kate said. As he left the stage, she turned to Ashley. "What is the matter with you?" she demanded. "Do you have something against Alex?"

"No," Ashley replied. "I just think he seems a little full of himself, that's all."

"Well, *I* think he's nice," Mary-Kate snapped. "If you want to help me out here, just keep your mouth shut, please."

Ashley sighed. "Sorry," she said.

Mary-Kate called the next boy.

After hearing eight more singers, Mary-Kate began to worry. So far, the only decent performer was Alex. Then the next boy came up—Jesse Bates.

"Hi, MK," he said as he stood on the stage.

Mary-Kate grinned at her friend. "Hi, Jesse. You ready?"

Jesse nodded and turned on the CD player. A hip-hop song blasted out. Jesse began to sing—and Mary-Kate's heart sank.

He was terrible. He mumbled the words, sang totally off-key, and couldn't even keep the beat.

Poor Jesse, she thought. *He's making an idiot of himself!*

When the song was over, Jesse bowed. Mary-Kate plastered a smile on her face and thanked him. She glanced at Ashley, who just shrugged.

Mary-Kate barely heard the next boy's audition. She was too worried about Jesse.

He's an awful singer, she thought. *But he's my friend. He'll be so hurt if I don't pick him to be in the group! But if I do, he'll ruin it for everyone!*

What should I do?

CHAPTER SIX

"You want to come to the mall with me and Hannah this afternoon?" Ashley asked Mary-Kate the next day at school. She tugged on the waistband of her bike shorts. "I want to get a riding outfit."

"A riding outfit!" Mary-Kate couldn't believe it. "But we don't have a horse."

"I know," Ashley said. She straightened the bill of her biker's cap. "But nobody else knows that."

Mary-Kate shook her head. "I can't go. I've got more auditions this afternoon. It's going to take days to see all those guys."

"Oh, right. The auditions," Ashley said. "Maybe I'll stop by and see how they're going."

"Great—as long as you're not riding in the Tour de France," Mary-Kate joked.

"I'm hitting the gym to lift some weights," Ashley said. "Later."

"Later," Mary-Kate said. She turned a corner and started walking toward her English class. Alex Marks was headed in her direction.

There he is, she thought, her heart racing. *I wonder if he'll stop to talk to me.*

"Mary-Kate!" he called. "I've been looking for you." He stopped and leaned against the wall next to her.

"You have?" Mary-Kate's voice came out squeaky.

"Yeah. I've got something I want to ask you."

"What is it?" The suspense made her want to clutch her stomach.

"Would you like to go to the dance with me?" Alex asked.

A voice inside Mary-Kate's head began to scream with excitement. *I can't believe it! I can't believe it!*

"Uhhh," she began. She couldn't seem to get any words out. At that moment David Jorgensen saw her and waved.

"Mary-Kate," David said, coming over. "I need to ask you something. It's about the dance."

"Hey, she's talking to *me* right now, David," Alex said. "You can ask her whatever it is when we're finished. Do you mind?"

"Hey—" David protested.

"Mary-Kate!" Jake O'Harrow said, running up. "I've been looking all over for you! I have a question. Will you go to the dance with me?"

"Well, I—" Mary-Kate looked from one boy to the other. What was going on? Alex had asked her first—and she definitely wanted to go with him. But as she stood surrounded by three boys, all of them eagerly waiting for her to choose between them, she started to feel confused.

"Come on, Mary-Kate," Alex said. "I asked you first."

Something kept Mary-Kate from answering right away. She felt overwhelmed by all the sudden attention. And she couldn't help wondering why all these boys were asking her to the dance. Could it have anything to do with the Cyberpunks?

"Um, can I think about it, guys?" she said. "I promise I'll give you an answer soon."

The boys' faces fell. She could see they were all disappointed. Then Alex brightened. "Sure," he said in a casual voice. "Whatever you want. I'll wait for your answer—MK."

Mary-Kate blushed. He'd never even spoken to her until a few days ago. Now he was calling her MK!

Alex must know he's a shoo-in for the band, she thought. *He doesn't need to butter me up. I think he really likes me. He just never noticed me before.*

"I'll wait, too," Jake promised.

"Me three," David said. "Take your time."

"Thanks, guys." Mary-Kate began to move away toward her English class.

"Oh, Mary-Kate," David called. "Have you made any decisions about the Cyberpunks yet?"

The other two boys stopped and perked up their ears.

"Not yet," Mary-Kate replied. "I still have a lot of people to audition. I'll let you know as soon as I decide."

"That's cool," David said. "I was just wondering, you know....No big deal or anything."

Wow, Mary-Kate thought as she walked away. *Just the other day I didn't have a clue who would ask me to the dance. Now it looks as though I can go with anybody I want!*

Rick stopped Ashley in the hall after history class. "You want to go to Raoul's for pizza tonight?" he asked her. "I need to talk to you about something."

"Pizza? Tonight?" Ashley repeated. "I don't think I can," she said shaking her head. "Tomorrow's the track team tryouts." Ashley was hoping to make track team. She hadn't practiced running as much as she'd meant to. But at least she knew better than to fill up on pizza the night before.

"So?" Rick asked.

"Well, I'm trying out for the team," Ashley told him.

Rick shot her a funny look. "You are?" he asked. "Really? The track team?"

Ashley nodded.

"Since when are you interested in track?" he asked. "And why are you wearing a bike-racing outfit?"

"Well, you see…" Ashley wasn't sure what to say. She had a feeling Rick sensed that she wasn't quite being herself. "I've always been kind of a jock, you know? I guess you just never noticed before."

Rick looked stung. "Oh. Okay. Fine. I guess we can talk another night." He turned and walked away.

Is he mad at me? Ashley wondered. *Oh, well. When we're the King and Queen of Cyberspace, he'll forget all about it.*

She headed to the cafeteria for lunch. She spotted Jake O'Harrow and Kevin Bly sitting together at a table and marched over to them. She had an idea.

"You guys are trying out for the Cyberpunks, aren't you?" she asked them.

The boys nodded. "I can't wait till that record

producer hears me sing," Jake said very seriously. "I've always known that I'd be a star. Now's my big chance to be discovered."

"I know what you mean, man," Kevin said. "Like, it's my fate, you know?"

"Uh, I'm sure it is," Ashley said. "You know, the whole thing rests in Mary-Kate's hands. She's *my sister*, remember? You know what I'm saying?"

"You and Mary-Kate are related?" Kevin turned to Jake, pretending to seem surprised. "Dude, did you know that?"

Jake rolled his eyes. "Ashley, are you saying you can help us?"

Ashley nodded. "Exactly. Mary-Kate really listens to me. She pretty much does whatever I tell her to. And if I tell her you're a Cyberpunk—you're a Cyberpunk."

"Excellent," Kevin said.

"You'd do that for us?" Jake asked.

"Sure," Ashley told him. *If I keep doing this, I'll get the vote of every guy in school!* she added to herself. *I'm so brilliant!*

Someone tapped her on the shoulder. Ashley whirled around to see a pretty red-haired girl named Jenna Jansen scowling at her.

"So, it's all *your* fault!" Jenna snapped.

"What's all my fault?" Ashley asked.

"The dance," Jenna said. "None of us girls has a date yet. All the boys want to be in that stupid boy band—so they're all asking your sister to the dance!"

"They are?" Ashley glanced back at Jake and Kevin. The two of them had slipped out of their seats and were slinking away.

"Yes, they are," Jenna said. She put her hands on her hips. "And I just caught you encouraging them. I'm going to tell everyone that it's your fault we don't have dates for the dance!"

"No!" Ashley cried. "Don't do that! It's not my fault—I swear! I've got nothing to do with it!"

"You said yourself that Mary-Kate will do whatever you tell her to," Jenna said. "If you want to be Queen of Cyberspace, tell her to hurry up and choose a date—or not one single girl will vote for you. And without the female vote there's no way you can win."

She stalked away to join a table full of girls. All the girls glared at Ashley.

Ashley swallowed hard. *Why does this Queen stuff have to be so complicated?*

CHAPTER SEVEN

Mary-Kate left the auditorium after another long afternoon of auditions. Most of the boys had been terrible, but a few had been pretty good. Another day or two and she'd be ready to choose the singers.

At least it will be easier than choosing a date for the dance, Mary-Kate thought. Five more boys had asked her to the dance that afternoon. They were all being so nice to her lately, and she had to admit she liked it. But she knew that some of them just wanted her to pick them for the group. *How can I tell who really likes me?* she wondered. *And who's just buttering me up?*

As she passed the gym, the door opened. Jesse stepped out, freshly showered after soccer practice. He stumbled, tripping over one of his shoelaces, but quickly recovered.

"MK," he said, grinning sheepishly. "I'm glad I ran into you. I've got a present for you."

He reached into his pocket and pulled out a tiny envelope.

"What is it?" Mary-Kate asked, taking the envelope.

"You'll see."

Mary-Kate opened the envelope and dumped the contents into her palm. Two small, round, spongy-looking things fell out. She glanced at Jesse, confused.

"I see them, but I still don't know what they are," she said.

"They're earplugs!" Jesse explained. "For the auditions. Just pop them in and no one will know you're not really listening!"

Mary-Kate laughed. "Thanks, Jesse. You have no idea how useful these will be. Some of those guys—" She paused, remembering how badly Jesse had sung. "Well, you know..." she finished, not sure what to say next.

"Remember the Blue Ponies?" Jesse said.

Mary-Kate smiled. One summer, when she and Jesse were seven years old, they'd started their own band called the Blue Ponies. Jesse played toy guitar and Mary-Kate played toy piano. They gave a concert in Jesse's backyard one day for Ashley and their parents.

"We thought we were going to be famous," Mary-Kate remembered. "We sang that song you made up, 'No Nose-Pickers in My Tree House.' "

Jesse cracked up. "Hey, that song was a classic."

He stopped at the bike rack and unlocked his bike. "You walking home?" he asked.

She nodded. Jesse's house was in the opposite direction from hers.

"You want to come over to my house?" he asked her. "We could work on our science projects. My mom can drive you home later."

"No, thanks," Mary-Kate replied. "I've got some stuff to do at home." She had to start going through her notes from the auditions—and she didn't want anyone else around while she was doing it.

"Okay." Jesse hopped on his bike. "See you tomorrow."

"See you!" Mary-Kate waved as he rode off down the street. She started walking in the other direction. She hadn't gone far when someone called out to her.

"Mary-Kate—wait up!" Alex ran to catch up with her. "Can I walk you home?"

Mary-Kate smiled. She'd thought Alex was cute ever since she'd first seen him two years ago. *And now he's finally noticed me,* she thought. *Even if he does want to be in the Cyberpunks. That doesn't mean he can't sincerely like me for myself, too—does it?*

"Hey, I don't want to pressure you or anything," Alex said. "But I really do want to take you to the dance. I don't know if those other guys are serious about it." He paused and brushed his hair away from his face. His green eyes burned into Mary-Kate's. "But I am."

Mary-Kate's breath stuck in her throat. She couldn't believe this was actually happening to her.

Alex took her hands in his. "Please," he said. "Give me your answer soon. I don't know how long I can stand to wait. If you don't want to go with me, I'll understand. But if you turn me down, I'll have to go to the dance alone. There's no other girl for me."

"Wow," Mary-Kate said, feeling stunned. "Um, all right, Alex. I'll try to make up my mind soon. I'm sorry to make you wait. It's just that there's so much going on right now."

"I understand," he said.

Mary-Kate stopped in front of her house. "Thanks for walking me home."

"No problem. See you tomorrow, MK."

She stood on the front porch for a few minutes, just watching Alex stroll down the street. *You know you want to go to the dance with him,* she told herself. *So why don't you just say yes?* But something was holding her back. She didn't know what it was.

Mary-Kate ran inside the house and upstairs to her room. She dumped her books on her desk and turned on her computer to check her E-mail. Piglet, the cat, rubbed against her legs and jumped into her lap.

"You've got mail," the computer chimed.

"Excellent," Mary-Kate said. She deleted some spam and stopped at a message from "Niceguy." *Who's that?* she wondered.

She opened the message.

FROM: NICEGUY
SUBJECT: YOU

YOU'RE A BRAVE GIRL TO SIT THROUGH ALL THOSE HOURS OF AUDITIONS. YOUR COURAGE IN THE FACE OF BAD SINGING IS AN INSPIRATION TO US ALL.

I WISH I WAS AS BRAVE AS YOU, MARY-KATE—BRAVE ENOUGH TO ASK YOU TO THE FALL DANCE, I MEAN. THE TROUBLE IS, I THINK I USED UP ALL MY COURAGE WHEN I SANG IN FRONT OF YOU. AND YOU'RE ALWAYS SUR-ROUNDED BY GUYS. YOU CAN GO TO THE DANCE WITH ANYBODY YOU WANT. SO I THINK I'LL JUST LET YOU KNOW THAT SOMEBODY REALLY LIKES YOU.

—A SECRET ADMIRER

CHAPTER EIGHT

"A secret admirer!" Mary-Kate gasped. "Who could it be?"

She read and reread the E-mail, searching for clues. She knew it was a boy who had auditioned for the group. *Maybe it's a joke,* she thought. *But if it's not...* A tingle of excitement ran through her.

If the message wasn't a joke, then whoever wrote it must really like her, she realized. She thought of all the boys who'd asked her to the dance already. They were all guys who wanted her to choose them for the Cyberpunks. But "Niceguy," whoever he was, was anonymous. Sending the E-mail wouldn't help him get into the boy band.

Could it be Alex? she wondered. *He was so sweet to walk me home today.* She'd been planning to tell Alex she'd go to the dance with him. But now...*I'd better wait and see who Niceguy is first,* she decided. She didn't want to make a mistake and go with the wrong guy.

"Mary-Kate? You have to let me in!" Ashley

knocked loudly on her bedroom door.

"It's open," Mary-Kate said just as Ashley burst through the door. "What's the matter?"

Ashley plopped down on Mary-Kate's bed. "Mary-Kate, have you decided who you're going to the dance with yet?" she demanded.

"Not yet," Mary-Kate began. "I just got this E-mail—"

"Well, hurry up!" Ashley cried. "You're ruining my chances of becoming Queen!"

"What are you talking about?" Mary-Kate asked.

"All the girls are mad at us because the boys won't ask them to the dance," Ashley explained. "The boys all want to be in your boy band, so they're all asking you! Jenna Jansen told me today that if you don't make up your mind, none of the girls will vote for me!"

"I'll decide soon," Mary-Kate promised. "I just have to find out something first." *If Alex is Niceguy,* she thought, *then I'll know for sure that he really likes me!*

Ashley met Hannah in the girls' locker room after track tryouts the next morning.

"How did it go?" Hannah asked, changing out of her leotard. Hannah was on the gymnastics team.

"Not so great," Ashley admitted. "We had to run fifty yards as fast as we could. The coach timed us. My time was the third slowest. Out of twenty-six."

"You didn't make the team?" Hannah said.

"No. And the worst part was, Kelly was there, helping the coach. She doesn't have to try out, of course. She wrote down everyone's time and read them out loud. I swear she started laughing when she read my time."

Hannah patted Ashley on the back. "There are other sports, you know. You don't have to be a track star just because Kelly is."

"I know," Ashley replied. "That's why I'm changing out of my track suit and into this." She held up a sparkly figure skater's costume.

Hannah snatched it out of her hands. "Oh, no, you're not," she said. "Anything but that. It's way overboard."

"Okay," Ashley agreed. "How about this soccer jersey? Everyone loves soccer."

Hannah sighed. "Fine."

"For your homework assignment this weekend, I want you all to write a short essay," Ms. Dubowski, Ashley's English teacher, told their class. Everyone groaned.

Ashley glanced across the room at Rick. He was eyeing her soccer outfit. Then he gave her a funny look.

What's his problem? Ashley wondered. *Hasn't he ever seen a soccer player before?*

"It's no big deal," Ms. Dubowski was saying about the homework. "Just two pages."

When the class ended and the students filed out of the classroom, Rick stopped Ashley in the hall-way.

"Want to work on our English essays together?" he asked. He and Ashley often studied together, writing out their essays and then reading them to each other.

Ashley frowned. The last of the singing auditions were being held that afternoon, and she didn't want to miss them. A lot of boys were going to be there—and she wanted to get them to vote for her. But she couldn't tell that to Rick.

"Um, I can't this afternoon," she said. "I'm—um—training for the triathlon."

Rick looked angry. Ashley could tell he didn't believe her. "All right, Ashley," he said. "I guess you have better things to do." He walked away.

He doesn't really want a girl who goes to the library and studies, Ashley thought as she watched him. *He wants a superjock, like Kelly.*

When school ended, Ashley hurried to the auditorium for the auditions. Mary-Kate sat in the front row, looking frazzled. Ashley sat next to her.

"Did I miss anything?" Ashley asked.

Mary-Kate nodded. "Joseph Serio sang a Green Day song—in his opera voice."

"Oooh." Ashley made a face.

As the parade of band-member hopefuls filed across the stage, Ashley found her mind wandering. She thought about how much fun she and Rick used to have doing homework together.

I wonder if he went to the library without me, she thought. *Maybe he's still there.*

"Sorry, I have to leave," she whispered to Mary-Kate. Ashley hurried out of the auditorium, across the courtyard, and back into the main building.

She pulled open the library door. The library was nearly empty. But Ashley spotted Rick at a table in the corner, half hidden by a tall bookcase.

He's still here! she thought happily. She headed for the table—and then stopped short.

Rick was writing his essay. But he wasn't alone.

Ashley's heart leaped to her throat. *I don't believe it,* she thought.

Sitting beside him was Kelly Benton!

CHAPTER NINE

"Kelly!" Ashley gasped. How could this be happening? Kelly and Rick...together. Kelly was taking Ashley's place!

Ashley stood frozen in place for a few seconds. Then she turned and stormed out of the library.

"Ashley, wait!" Rick ran after her.

Ashley burst through the front doors, out into the sunny afternoon. She ran down the front steps. Rick hurried after her and looped around in front of her, blocking her way.

"Ashley, listen!" he cried.

"What are you doing with Kelly?" Ashley demanded. She was so hurt and upset she was afraid she'd start crying. But she didn't want to do that—not there, not right in front of him.

"We're just studying," Rick insisted. "We were working on our English essays. That's all."

"That's *all*? But that's our thing! Our thing that *we* do together! Kelly's been scheming to get you back ever since you broke up with her, and you know it!"

"We're just friends," Rick said. "Whether you believe me or not. At this point I don't know if I even care what you think. You've been acting pretty weird lately, Ashley. What's up with you?"

"I don't know what you're talking about," Ashley said.

"You keep making up excuses not to see me," Rick said. "You're always pretending to be on the track team or the soccer team. But I know that's not the real you. When did you become Ms. Superjock?"

Ashley bristled. She was doing it all for him—didn't he understand that?

She took a deep breath, trying to calm herself down. Then, in the coldest voice she could muster, she said, "If you don't like superjocks, then why are you hanging out with Kelly?"

Ashley didn't wait for an answer. She stormed off, furious. Once she reached the street, she ran all the way home.

The auditions were almost over, but Mary-Kate had barely heard the last few boys sing. Instead she'd been thinking about her secret admirer. She had studied each boy carefully, looking for clues. Could Joseph be Niceguy? What about David? Jake?

I should just forget about it, she thought. *The*

message was probably a joke, anyway.

After the last boy sang, Mary-Kate made a note on her clipboard. "Okay, that's it," she announced. "Thank you all ior trying out. I'll post the names of the group members as soon as I know them."

She picked up her backpack and started to leave. Boys crowded around her.

"Do you have any idea who *might* make it?" one boy asked.

"Can't you just give us a hint?" another begged.

"No!" Mary-Kate said firmly. She managed to break away from the pack of boys and hurried home.

Mary-Kate slipped into her room, closed the door, and turned on the computer. As she waited for the Internet to log on, she realized her pulse was racing again. Had Niceguy written her another note?

"You've got mail," the computer chimed.

There it was. A message from Niceguy. Mary-Kate quickly opened it.

HEY, CUTIE—WHAT'S UP WITH YOUR SISTER? DID SHE HAVE A PERSONALITY TRANSPLANT OR SOMETHING? MAYBE IT'S JUST THE DANCE THING—IT'S TURNING THE WHOLE SCHOOL UPSIDE DOWN. KIDS COMPETING TO RULE CYBERSPACE—WHATEVER THAT MEANS—AND TRY-

ING TO BE THE NEXT POP STAR. HAS THE WHOLE WORLD
GONE CRAZY?

THE ANSWER IS YES. EVEN I'VE GONE CRAZY—CRAZY
OVER YOU.

YOUR SECRET ADMIRER,
NICEGUY

"Who *is* this?" Mary-Kate squealed. She clicked
Reply and wrote:

NICEGUY—I LIKE YOUR E-MAILS. PLEASE TELL ME WHO
YOU ARE. WHY ARE YOU KEEPING YOUR IDENTITY A
SECRET?

MARY-KATE

She pressed Send and waited. *I hope he's on-line
now,* she thought. *I can't wait for him to write back!*

Nothing happened for several minutes. Mary-
Kate began to get restless. *Come on, come on!* she
thought, tapping her computer. *Answer me!*

At last, a message popped up. *Please be from
Niceguy,* she thought. It was!

I'M SORRY. I CAN'T TELL YOU WHO I AM. YOU'D PROBA-
BLY LAUGH YOUR HEAD OFF IF YOU KNEW. AND YOU JUST
WOULDN'T BE AS CUTE WITHOUT A HEAD.

I won't laugh! Mary-Kate thought. *I promise I won't!* She read the rest of the message.

MAYBE I'LL ASK YOU OUT LATER, ONCE THIS DANCE CRAZINESS DIES DOWN. BUT FOR NOW, LIKE BATMAN, I'VE GOT TO KEEP MY TRUE IDENTITY A SECRET. YOU UNDERSTAND, DON'T YOU, BATGIRL?

What a funny guy, Mary-Kate thought with a sigh. *If only he'd tell me who he is! I know I'd like him!*

I'll find out somehow, she vowed. *No secret is safe from me!*

Ashley stayed in her room all evening. That night she tossed and turned, unable to sleep.

Maybe I've played this campaign all wrong, she thought miserably. *I've been trying so hard to be as popular as Kelly that I forgot why I wanted to be Queen in the first place—to be with Rick! Now Rick is mad at me. Maybe he hates me!*

Worst of all, he was hanging out with Kelly again. What if they got back together?

Maybe it's not too late, Ashley thought. *Whatever happens, I can't let Kelly win!*

• • •

It rained all weekend. Mary-Kate and Ashley spent Saturday and Sunday stuck inside the house. Mary-Kate paced back and forth, hoping for more E-mails from her secret admirer. But none came.

Ashley sulked over Rick the whole time. Mary-Kate tried to cheer her up with a board game, but Mystery Date didn't work.

"You're taking this too hard," Mary-Kate told her sister. "All Rick and Kelly were doing was sitting at a table in the library together. I study with Jesse all the time. That doesn't mean we're going out."

"You don't know Kelly," Ashley insisted. "If she wants something, she doesn't give up until she gets it. And she wants Rick."

On Monday morning Mary-Kate was glad to see Ashley dressed as her old self instead of some kind of Olympic athlete. "No more superjock?" she asked.

"I've given up on that," Ashley admitted. "It wasn't working for me. But I still want to win Queen of Cyberspace."

As soon as she walked into school, Mary-Kate was surrounded by boys.

"So who made the group, Mary-Kate?" David asked.

"Are you posting the list today?" Joseph said.

A boy whose name she couldn't remember

demanded, "Who are you going to the dance with?"

"Everybody calm down!" Mary-Kate shouted. Then she realized something. Now was her chance to expose her secret admirer! She studied the faces of the dozens of boys around her.

"Kevin," she said slowly, "do you like to *boogie*?" She watched his reaction carefully.

"What? Do we have to dance, too?" Kevin cried. "You never said that!"

"No, no. Never mind." Maybe this wasn't such a good idea. Frustrated, she pushed her way through the mob and headed for her locker.

A boy named Jim Barber had the locker next to hers. He was a quiet guy. Mary-Kate had never paid much attention to him until he'd auditioned for the Cyberpunks.

I hope he's not Niceguy, she thought. *But it could be anybody. Let me try again.*

"Hi, Jim." Mary-Kate looked him right in the eye and smiled. Jim seemed surprised that she was even talking to him.

"Uh, hi, Mary-Kate," he said.

Mary-Kate noticed that he was holding a book they were reading for English class. "So how do you like *The Heart Is a Lonely Hunter*?" she asked him.

"Uh, how d-d-do I like it?" Jim stammered. He

seemed nervous. "It's okay, I guess."

"Don't you think it should be called something different, like, say, *The Heart Is a Lonely NICEGUY?*" she asked, wiggling her eyebrows.

Jim looked confused. "Um, sure, if you say so. Anyway, I'll see you in class." He hurried away.

Mary-Kate sighed. She knew she'd never find out who Niceguy was at this rate.

The lunch line was long at the cafeteria that afternoon. Mary-Kate sighed again as she stood at the end, waiting for it to move. It was pizza day, and they seemed to have temporarily run out.

"The food here's not worth the wait," a voice behind her said. Mary-Kate turned to see Alex standing behind her.

"Hey," she said, smiling shyly.

"I know a place where the pizza's really great," he said. "And you don't even have to wait in line for it."

"Where's that?" Mary-Kate asked.

"Mario's," Alex said. "Brick-oven pizza. Want to go there with me sometime?"

"Sure." Mary-Kate blushed. Was he asking her out on a date?

"How about tomorrow night?"

"Tomorrow night's great!" Mary-Kate replied.

"I'll pick you up at your house at seven," Alex

said. He grinned and walked away.

Mary-Kate couldn't stand waiting in the line any longer. She had to look for Ashley. She couldn't wait to tell her the news. Alex Marks had asked her out!

Maybe this is the sign I've been looking for, she thought. *Alex must be Niceguy!*

"Ashley wants to be Queen of Cyberspace," Mary-Kate said between bites of brick-oven pizza. Tuesday night had finally arrived and she was out to dinner with Alex. "That's why she's been acting so weird lately. I don't think she really cares about winning. She just doesn't want somebody else to win. Her boyfriend, Rick, is running for King."

"I'll vote against him if you want. If he loses, your sister will have nothing to worry about." Alex was staring just past Mary-Kate's shoulder. She turned and looked at the wall behind her. There was a mirror hanging right behind her head. *He's not even looking at me,* she thought, annoyed. *He's staring at himself in the mirror!*

"Do you have any brothers or sisters?" she asked, trying to steer his attention back to her.

"An older brother and an older sister," he replied. "My brother's in New York, trying to become an actor. He's got an agent and everything.

His agent says it's only a matter of time before he's a star."

"Wow," Mary-Kate said. "And what about your sister?"

"She's in college. She plays bass in a band there. They're *this close* to getting a record deal." He held his thumb and forefinger about an inch apart.

"Talented family." Mary-Kate nodded politely, but she felt a little overwhelmed. "So I guess it makes sense that you'd want to be a singer."

"Exactly." Alex was looking right in her eyes at last. "I think I've got what it takes, you know?" he said. "I'm going to be famous one day. The sooner the better."

Mary-Kate finished her pizza. She had to admit Alex *was* talented. And he'd had more stage presence than any other guy at the auditions. But Ashley was right—if only he weren't so *conceited* about it....

Alex glanced around the room. "Hey, there's Kelly Benton," he said, nodding in the direction of a corner table.

Mary-Kate turned and saw Kelly sitting with three of her friends. The girls were talking and laughing loudly.

"They were actually wearing stonewashed

denim," Kelly said, making fun of someone. "Can you believe it? It was so eighties! But not in a good way."

I'm so glad Ashley's not trying to be like Kelly anymore, Mary-Kate thought.

"She sure is a cool girl," Alex said. "Are you friends with her?"

"Not really," Mary-Kate admitted.

"Oh. Do you think she saw me?"

"I don't know, Alex. Why don't you go over and say hi to her?"

"Maybe on our way out. Hey, isn't she running against your sister Andrea for the cyberqueen thing?"

"Ashley," Mary-Kate corrected. "My sister's name is Ashley."

When the evening was over, Alex stood on Mary-Kate's front porch and sang a few lines to her. "It's so hard to say good-bye, girl...."

Mary-Kate tried to smile. Alex really did have a good voice. She just hadn't had a very good time with him.

He leaned down and kissed her on the cheek. "See you tomorrow."

"Okay," Mary-Kate said. "Good night." She went inside and straight up to her room. Ashley was waiting for her there, dying to hear all about the date.

Mary-Kate filled her in as she changed into her pajamas. "Alex was nice," she said. "Just...oh, I don't know. Niceguy seems so much more fun...."

She logged on to the Internet to check her E-mail. Her heart pounded when she saw a message from Niceguy.

HEY, MISS POPULARITY—THOSE GUYS ARE REALLY HOUNDING YOU! YOU DIDN'T LOOK VERY HAPPY ABOUT IT, THOUGH. DON'T LET THEM GET TO YOU. THE MARY-KATE I KNOW IS VERY HONEST AND ALWAYS DOES THE RIGHT THING. THAT'S WHAT'S SO COOL ABOUT YOU.

"Wow," Ashley breathed, reading over Mary-Kate's shoulder. "Who *is* this guy?"

Mary-Kate frowned. "That's what I would like to know."

CHAPTER TEN

"Sorry, but I can't go to the dance with any of you," Mary-Kate told the crowd of boys who mobbed her the next morning.

The boys groaned. "Why not, Mary-Kate?" one of them asked.

"Because I can't tell if any of you are sincere," she told them. "I want to go with someone who really likes me for myself—not because they want me to help make them famous."

"I like you for yourself—*really*!" Kevin insisted.

Mary-Kate rolled her eyes. "It doesn't matter, anyway," she said. "Because I've already chosen the Cyberpunks. Their names are on this piece of paper."

She rattled a piece of loose-leaf paper. The boys and a crowd of other students crowded around to hear the names.

"Jake O'Harrow, Michael Woolsey, Chris Preston, Rasheed Phillips, and Alex Marks," Mary-Kate announced. "You were all great," she lied. "I wish I could have chosen all of you."

Our school is gearing up for the biggest dance of the year: Cyberdance!

Next on the agenda? Dates! Ashley's sure her boyfriend, Rick, will ask her. But who am I going to go with?

Betsy put us in charge of auditions for a boy band to sing at the dance. That made us pretty popular!

We had a blast decorating the gym for the big night.

Ashley went a little crazy during her campaign to become Queen of Cyberspace. Then Rick wasn't sure he wanted to be her date anymore. Yikes!

I ended up going to the dance with Jesse, my best friend (soon to be my boyfriend?). He's a great dancer!

Ashley and Rick made up at the dance. Aren't they cute together?

Let's hear it for happy endings!

The boys who weren't chosen began to walk away, grumbling. "Meet with Mr. Moreland after school today for your first rehearsal," Mary-Kate called out over the dispersing crowd. "We'll see you at the dance a week from Friday!"

Alex rushed over to her. "Thanks, Mary-Kate," he said.

"I didn't choose you because you asked me out, Alex," she said. "I chose you because you're talented."

"I know. Thanks," he said again. "Once that record producer sees me, I'll be on my way!" Then he ran down the hall, whooping with excitement.

As the crowd thinned out, she spotted Jesse lingering by the water fountain. He gazed up at her for a few seconds, then smiled and gave her a little wave.

Mary-Kate smiled back stiffly. She was afraid his feelings might be hurt because she hadn't chosen him for the band. *Should I go over and say something to him?* she wondered. But before she had a chance to decide, Jesse turned and walked away.

Mary-Kate bit her lip. She felt terrible. She wished she could have picked Jesse. But he was such a terrible singer! It just wouldn't have been right.

I hope he doesn't take this personally, she thought sadly. *I hope he'll still be friends with me.*

The rest of the day was the quietest Mary-Kate had had in more than a week. The boys stopped hounding her now that the contest was over. Most of them stopped paying attention to her.

"Now I don't have a date at all," she told Ashley as they walked home that afternoon. "I guess that was stupid of me."

"Someone nice will ask you," Ashley said. They went inside the house and headed upstairs to Mary-Kate's room.

"You know what? I'm sick of waiting around for the right guy to ask me," Mary-Kate said. She sat at her desk and flipped her computer on.

Ashley watched her. "What are you doing?"

"I'm going to write to my secret admirer and ask *him* to the dance," Mary-Kate declared.

"What?" Ashley was horrified. "But you don't even know who he is!"

"Well, I know he's a nice guy," Mary-Kate replied, shrugging. "And I know he likes me."

"But he could be anybody!" Ashley cried.

"I'll take that chance," Mary-Kate said. She began to type an E-mail.

DEAR NICEGUY,
    WELL, SECRET ADMIRER, YOUR PLAN WORKED. I

DON'T KNOW WHO YOU ARE, BUT I'M DYING TO FIND OUT. SO I FIGURE, NOW'S MY CHANCE! AS IT TURNS OUT, I DON'T HAVE A DATE FOR THE DANCE. I'M SURE THAT SOMEONE AS SWEET AND FUNNY AS YOU ARE ALREADY HAS A DATE. BUT ON THE SMALL CHANCE THAT YOU DON'T—WOULD YOU LIKE TO GO WITH ME?

WRITE BACK SOON.

She pressed Send. Then she sat back and grinned at her sister.

"I can't believe you just did that," Ashley said.

Five minutes later Mary-Kate had an E-mail. "It's from Niceguy!" she told Ashley. "This is it!"

She nervously opened the message. It said:

YOU'RE IN LUCK, MARY-KATE. I WAS GOING TO TAKE MY MOTHER TO THE DANCE, BUT SHE TURNED ME DOWN. THAT MEANS I'M FREE! AND I'D LOVE TO GO WITH YOU. OF COURSE, I'D RATHER GO WITH MY MOTHER, BUT WHAT CAN YOU DO? (SERIOUSLY, YOU ARE SO COOL TO ASK ME.)

I'LL PICK YOU UP AT YOUR HOUSE AT SEVEN ON FRIDAY NIGHT. I CAN'T WAIT. I JUST HOPE YOU WON'T BE DISAP-POINTED WHEN YOU SEE ME.

"So do I," Mary-Kate said, gulping.

CHAPTER ELEVEN

"Now that you have your answer, Mary-Kate," Ashley said, "would you please stop hogging the phone line? I need to send E-mails to everybody in school to remind them to vote for me."

"It's all yours," Mary-Kate said.

Ashley sat at her desk and logged on. Piglet jumped into her lap. Ashley used the Fleming High network to enter the E-mail address of every student. Then she hesitated, wondering what to write.

She fiddled with a few drafts, but nothing seemed quite right. Frustrated, she began tapping out whatever came into her mind.

KELLY BENTON KELLY BENTON KELLY BENTON KELLY BENTON IS A BIG FAKE. SHE THINKS SHE'S COOL BUT SHE'S NOT. SHE'S NOT EVEN PRETTY. KELLY BENTON IS BALD AND WEARS A WIG. KELLY BENTON CAN'T GET A DATE. THAT'S WHY SHE HAS TO STEAL OTHER PEOPLE'S BOYFRIENDS....

As she typed, venting her anger at Kelly, Ashley

began to feel better. She was still writing insults when Piglet jumped on the mouse.

"Piglet, get down from there!" Ashley cried. Then a little sign appeared on her screen: YOUR MESSAGE HAS BEEN SENT.

Ashley gasped. The mouse had been pointed to Send! Piglet had just sent all those insults about Kelly to everybody in school!

"Piglet!" she cried again. The cat leaped off the desk and settled on the bed.

"I don't believe this," Ashley moaned. "I just insulted the most popular girl in school! I didn't want to hurt Kelly's feelings!" She quickly set up a new E-mail for everybody to read.

DEAR EVERYONE—THE LAST E-MAIL YOU GOT FROM ME WAS A BIG MISTAKE. I DIDN'T MEAN THE THINGS I WROTE AND I DIDN'T MEAN TO SEND THEM TO YOU—IT WAS AN ACCIDENT! I THINK KELLY BENTON IS A VERY PRETTY AND NICE GIRL AND SHE DOESN'T WEAR A WIG. I DON'T WANT TO HURT HER FEELINGS. PLEASE FORGIVE ME AND ACCEPT MY APOLOGIES!

I hope this works, Ashley thought as she sent the message. *Because if not, things are going to be pretty frosty at school tomorrow!*

• • •

"Hi, Betsy!" Ashley called to Betsy Browner as she arrived at school the next morning. Betsy, who was normally super-friendly, walked away from Ashley without a word. That was Ashley's first clue that her apology hadn't worked.

Kids turned away from her as she walked slowly down the hall to her locker. Even people she hardly knew threw her angry glares.

As she fiddled with the lock on her locker, Ashley spotted Rick coming her way. *Maybe he's not mad at me like the others,* she hoped.

She held her breath as Rick walked up to her and stopped. "How could you?" he demanded. "How could you do something so mean? Do you really want to be Queen of Cyberspace that badly?"

"N-no!" Ashley sputtered. "I didn't mean to do it! I apologized!"

"You still hurt Kelly's feelings," Rick said. "A lot." Ashley realized that she'd never thought of Kelly Benton as having feelings. She'd always seemed so perfect, as if nothing could hurt her.

"Rick—" Ashley began. She took a deep breath and plunged in. "Um, we're still going to the dance together...right?"

Rick shrugged. "Sorry," he said. "I've made

other plans. I've got to go now. Bye."

Ashley stared after him as he walked away, her heart in her throat. *Oh no,* she thought miserably. *Rick's taking someone else!*

"What were you thinking?" Hannah asked as Ashley sat next to her in science class. "You insult the most popular girl in school—by sending E-mails to everyone? Have you lost your mind?"

"Didn't anybody get my apology?" Ashley protested. "The whole thing was an accident. I just wanted to remind everybody to vote for me, but I started writing little mean things about Kelly because I was mad at her. And then Piglet sat on the mouse and sent it to the whole school! But I never meant to do it, I swear!" she cried, almost in tears.

Hannah touched her arm. "Don't worry. I believe you."

"Thanks," Ashley said. "But it doesn't matter. No one will vote for me now. And I've already lost Rick." She blinked back tears.

"I give up, Hannah," she sobbed. "I'm not going to the dance at all. I tried so hard to make everybody vote for me. And now, except for you and Mary-Kate, everybody hates me!"

CHAPTER TWELVE

"Ash-ley," Mary-Kate said in a singsong voice. "Look what I got for you." She held up a cool black party dress, trying to tempt her sister into putting it on. "Don't you want to go to the dance with me?"

Ashley sadly shook her head no.

It was the night of Cyberdance. Mary-Kate was already wearing her burgundy velvet dress and was ready to go. But she was nervous. She still didn't know who her date was.

"What if Niceguy doesn't show up?" Mary-Kate said. "Please, Ashley, I need you to come with me!"

"I can't," Ashley said. She lay in a pile of pillows on her bed, wearing her pajamas. "It's hard enough just going to school every day. How can I go to a dance where everybody hates me?"

"Everybody doesn't hate you," Mary-Kate said. "And I know Rick still likes you."

The doorbell rang. Mary-Kate froze.

"It's him, Ashley!" she cried.

"Good luck, Mary-Kate," Ashley said. She buried

her head under a mound of pink pillows.

As calmly as she could, Mary-Kate walked downstairs to the front door. She held the handle for a few seconds and took a deep breath. "Here goes," she murmured.

She threw open the door. There stood Hannah with two boys—her date, Daniel, and another boy Mary-Kate didn't know.

"Surprise!" Hannah said. "We've come to drag Ashley to the dance. She's going—even if we have to carry her in kicking and screaming. Mary-Kate, this is my cousin Walker. He can be Ashley's date."

Mary-Kate smiled and shook Walker's hand. Hannah's cousin was very cute—tall, short black hair, nice blue eyes, a sweet face.

"Good luck convincing her to go," Mary-Kate said as Hannah dashed upstairs to Ashley's room. Then Mary-Kate led Daniel and Walker to the living room and offered them sodas and snacks. "Have a seat, guys," she said. "This might take a while."

Ashley hid her head under a pillow when she saw Hannah. "Go away."

"Ashley, you have to go to the dance," Hannah said. "You have no choice. It's your duty as a candidate for Queen of Cyberspace."

"Nobody will vote for me," Ashley said.

"There's another reason you have to go—I brought you a date."

"Hannah, no!" Ashley shuddered. What kind of reject could Hannah scrounge up at the last minute? "I'm not ready for a new boyfriend."

"Good, because your date isn't available. He has a girlfriend."

"What?" Ashley glared at Hannah. "What are you trying to do to me?"

"Don't worry," Hannah said. "It's my cousin Walker. You remember him. He's in town visiting us for the weekend."

Ashley brightened. "The tall one?" Ashley had always thought Walker was cute.

"That's the one. He's always liked you and he thought it would be fun to go to the dance." Hannah grabbed Ashley by the arm and dragged her out of bed. "Hurry up and dress or we'll be late!"

Ashley felt a little better knowing that Hannah and Walker wanted to help her. She quickly put on the dress. Hannah helped her with her hair and makeup. They were ready in ten minutes.

"That must be a world record," Hannah said as they headed downstairs.

Walker stood up when Ashley entered the living

room. "Wow," he said. "You're even prettier than I remembered."

Ashley smiled. Maybe this dance wouldn't be so horrible after all.

The doorbell rang again. Mary-Kate jumped. Hannah and Ashley followed her to the door.

"Do you mind?" Mary-Kate said, shooing them back into the living room.

But Ashley and Hannah peeked out to watch.

Mary-Kate gulped and opened the door to meet her secret admirer. There stood a slender, brown-haired boy holding a bouquet of pink roses.

"Jesse!" she cried. "It's you! You're Niceguy?"

Jesse nodded. "You're not disappointed, are you?"

Mary-Kate threw her arms around his neck and gave him a hug. "No way. I'm so glad it's you!"

He handed her the flowers. "I've liked you for a long time, MK," he said. "But I was too shy to tell you."

"I've always liked you, too, Jesse," Mary-Kate said. "But until now, I never realized how much." She led him inside. "Hey, guys, look who it is!" she cried.

Ashley and Hannah cheered. Then Mary-Kate introduced Jesse to Walker and Daniel and the three couples happily set off for the dance.

Ashley gasped as she entered the gym. "Betsy really went all out for this," she said in amazement.

The room was dark and spacy-looking, filled with tiny blinking lights and mazes of colored computer wire. Computer terminals were set up near the entrance for E-mail, web surfing, and voting for the King and Queen of Cyberspace.

"Ugh," Ashley groaned to her sister. "Just seeing those computers makes me feel sick." She took Walker by the hand and said quickly, "Want to dance?"

"Sure," he said, and the two of them threaded their way through the crowd to the dance floor.

Ashley had just started dancing when her back bumped into someone. "Sorry," she said, turning to see whom she'd bumped. It was Rick—and he was dancing with Kelly!

He glanced at her, then at Walker. Then he grabbed Kelly's hand and stalked off the dance floor.

Ashley felt as if she'd been punched in the stomach. *I knew it!* she thought. *Rick's back together with Kelly!*

CHAPTER THIRTEEN

Ashley tried to put Rick out of her mind and focus on Walker. They danced for a while, but she couldn't stop worrying about Rick. When the song was over, she said, "Can you excuse me for a few minutes? I need to find somebody."

"No problem," Walker said. He joined Hannah and Daniel at a table while Ashley hurried away, looking for Rick.

She couldn't find him anywhere. *He must be avoiding me,* she thought. *But I've got to find him. I've got to make him understand how sorry I am about everything.*

Then she thought of a way she could reach him—his trusty Palm Pilot. She ran to one of the computers and typed an E-mail message.

RICK—I'M SO SORRY ABOUT EVERYTHING. I'M SORRY I HURT KELLY'S FEELINGS. I PROMISE I NEVER MEANT FOR THAT TO HAPPEN. AND I'M SORRY I ACTED LIKE SUCH A JERK TO YOU WHEN I WAS TRYING TO BE COOL. I WON'T

TRY TO BE SOMEONE I'M NOT ANYMORE, RICK. PLEASE
FORGIVE ME. —ASHLEY.

Crossing her fingers, she sent the message to
Rick's Palm Pilot and hoped for the best.

She found Walker waiting for her at their table
near the dance floor. Jesse and Mary-Kate were
dancing nearby. *Wow*, Ashley thought as she
watched them. *Jesse may be a terrible singer, but he
sure is a great dancer.* Mary-Kate was laughing as he
twirled her around. Ashley thought she'd never seen
her sister so happy. *At least one of us is having a
good time*, she told herself with a sigh.

An electronic board over the stage kept track of
the race for King and Queen of Cyberspace. Under
each candidate's name was a column showing how
many votes he or she had so far. Marie Duncan
updated the tallies every few minutes.

Ashley stared at the board. Rick was clearly in
the lead among the boys. But the girls' race was a
lot tighter. With almost two-thirds of the votes
counted, Kelly had fifty-four votes, but Ashley had
fifty and a third candidate, Diana Chandler, had
forty-eight. Ashley was amazed to see that she actually had a chance to win! Her apology must have
been accepted after all.

"Hannah told me there's supposed to be some kind of special guest DJ tonight," Walker said. "A record producer or something. Have you seen him?"

"No," Ashley replied. "But I think Betsy's going to introduce him soon."

A few minutes later Betsy ran up on stage. The music stopped. The dancers stopped dancing and turned to face the stage. An excited hush fell over the room.

"This is it," Ashley whispered to Walker. "She's going to bring out the special guest DJ."

"Thanks for coming to Cyberdance!" Betsy said. Everyone clapped and whooped. "It's a great success so far. And now, here's your special guest DJ!"

Ashley held her breath. Who would it be?

CHAPTER FOURTEEN

Mary-Kate felt the tension in the crowd as everyone waited to see who the guest DJ was. A short, bald, older man stepped onto the stage. He was carrying a baseball cap with moose ears on top of it.

If that's a record producer, I'm a nuclear physicist, Mary-Kate thought.

"And here he is," Betsy announced. "DJ Shinyhead! Otherwise known as my uncle Marty!"

"Good evening, ladies and germs!" Uncle Marty shouted. Then he darted over to the DJ booth and started spinning records. Music blasted out of the speakers, but no one danced.

"Hey!" someone shouted. "What's going on?"

"Yeah—where's the record producer?" another student called out.

Betsy spoke into her microphone. "Uncle Marty is the special guest DJ!" she explained. "He's not a record producer, but he has an awesome collection of tunes. Surprise!"

The crowd groaned with disappointment.

Mary-Kate was disappointed, too. She had really been hoping there would be a major celebrity at the party.

Uncle Marty ignored everybody and kept the beat going. Soon Mary-Kate found herself tapping her foot. She kept getting an irresistible urge to dance.

"I feel like dancing again," Jesse said.

"That's just what I was thinking!" Mary-Kate said.

A few minutes later the dance floor was packed with kids grooving to Betsy's uncle's cool music. Mary-Kate and Jesse danced next to Walker and Ashley.

"Shinyhead may not be famous!" Jesse shouted to Mary-Kate over the music. "But he's a great DJ!"

"I know!" Mary-Kate raised her arms in the air and twirled around. She was having an amazing time dancing with Jesse.

Finally the music stopped again. By then Mary-Kate was completely exhausted. She fell into a seat next to Jesse at their table. Soon Ashley and Walker and Hannah and Daniel joined them.

Crowds of kids lined up at the refreshment table for bottles of water. Then the electronic board tallying the votes for King and Queen went dark.

Mary-Kate watched Betsy step out from behind the DJ booth to center stage.

"Okay, you guys," Betsy said. "This is the moment you've all been waiting for. It's time to crown the King and Queen of Cyberspace! But first, I'd like to introduce Fleming's very own boy band, the Cyberpunks!" The five boy singers lined up next to Betsy.

Jesse leaned close to Mary-Kate. "Uh-oh," he whispered. "Did you bring your earplugs?"

Mary-Kate giggled.

Marie handed Betsy a piece of paper.

"Here we go," Betsy began. "The boy with the most votes and the King of Cyberspace is ... Rick Morgan!"

The audience whooped and clapped as Rick ran up on stage. Mary-Kate and Ashley clapped, too. They'd always known he'd win, but they were excited for him, anyway.

Ashley felt a pang as Betsy put a silly gold crown on Rick's head. He looked so cute! But he didn't look very happy.

"And now for the Queen," Betsy went on. "This was a tight race, as you all know." She paused.

Mary-Kate held her breath and glanced at her sister. Was there any chance that Ashley could win?

CHAPTER FIFTEEN

"And the Queen of Cyberspace is...Kelly Benton!" Betsy shouted.

Ashley's heart sank as the crowd cheered. She was disappointed, but definitely not surprised.

Kelly slowly made her way up to the stage. The Cyberpunks started singing a romantic song as Betsy placed a glittering tiara on Kelly's blond head. Kelly smiled and waved to the crowd.

"You should have won," Walker whispered to Ashley.

She smiled. "Thanks. But if you knew about some of the things I tried to do to win, you might not think so."

All eyes were on the stage as Betsy pushed Kelly and Rick together. "Dance!" she ordered. Over at the DJ booth, her uncle Marty played another slow song.

Rick took Kelly in his arms. As they started to sway, Kelly rested her head on Rick's shoulder. Ashley felt as if she were going to cry right there at the table. She jumped to her feet and bolted toward the bathroom.

"Ashley!"

She heard Walker call after her, but she didn't stop. She couldn't. It was too hard to watch Rick and Kelly together.

The girls' room was empty. Ashley sat on the floor behind the last stall as hot tears streamed down her face.

"Ashley?" Mary-Kate called.

"Are you in here?" she heard Hannah ask.

Ashley gasped, hoping they wouldn't notice her. She didn't feel like talking to anybody—not even her sister.

But Mary-Kate found her anyway. "Come out of there," she said gently, then pushed open the door. "Come on."

Ashley came out and sat on the windowsill, her face wet with tears. Mary-Kate and Hannah sat quietly on either side of her for a few seconds. Then Mary-Kate hugged her.

Ashley started sobbing again.

"Nobody really cares about this stupid Cyberspace royalty stuff," Hannah told her. "It's meaningless."

"And everybody's already forgotten all about

being mad at you," Mary-Kate said. "Did you see how many votes you got? You almost beat Kelly, even though you made a few silly mistakes. That shows how much everybody likes you."

"That E-mail you sent didn't really hurt anybody," Hannah added. "Kelly's as popular as ever. And you apologized right away."

"It's all behind us now," Mary-Kate said. "Everyone is having fun at the dance. That's all that matters. And you should have fun, too, Ashley. Walker's waiting for you."

Ashley wiped her tears away and smiled a little. It was great to have such an awesome sister. And a fantastic friend like Hannah.

"Come on, Ashley," Hannah urged her. "Let's get out there and dance!"

Ashley jumped off the windowsill. Mary-Kate and Hannah were right. "I'm going to have a good time tonight if it kills me," she vowed.

"That's the spirit!" Mary-Kate cheered. "I think."

The three girls returned to their table.

Then Ashley spotted Rick, hovering nearby. He held his crown in his hands, nervously tossing it from one hand to the other.

"Ashley, hi," he said quietly.

"Hi," she replied, wondering what Rick was

going to say next. She looked at the floor.

"I got your apology." He pulled his Palm Pilot out of his pocket to show her. "I was really glad. You were being so cold to me I thought you didn't like me anymore."

"Of course I like you," Ashley said. "I did all those stupid things *because* I like you. But I kind of got carried away. It all backfired, I guess." She sighed. "So where's your date?"

"My date?" Rick looked confused.

"Aren't you here with Kelly?" Ashley asked.

Rick shook his head. "She asked me to the dance the other day. But I didn't come with anybody."

"But you told me you had plans," Ashley said. Now she was the one who was confused.

"I did," Rick admitted. "I planned to come to the dance by myself. I didn't want to come with you, the way you were acting. But I didn't want to be with anybody else, either."

Ashley grinned. She was so relieved!

Rick took her hand and led her out on the dance floor. The Cyberpunks were singing a slow song. Rick placed his crown on top of Ashley's head and they started dancing.

"I don't care if Kelly was voted Queen of Cyberspace," he whispered in Ashley's ear.

"*You're* the only queen of my world."

Ashley smiled and held Rick close. It was good to be back to normal—her regular old self.

Mary-Kate spotted her sister and Rick together and steered Jesse across the dance floor.

"Looks like they're a couple again," she said to Jesse as they started to dance. She was so glad things were working out at last.

Jesse glanced back at the band on the stage. "You know, those guys aren't bad. You did a good job, MK."

"Thanks." She had to agree. The Cyberpunks were pretty good. Too bad there was no producer there to discover them.

They danced closer to Ashley and Rick. Mary-Kate grinned at her sister over Jesse's shoulder.

Ashley grinned back.

"Is everything okay?" Mary-Kate asked Ashley.

"Super-okay," Ashley replied.

Jesse kissed Mary-Kate's forehead to get her attention. "Hey, no talking to your sister," he joked. "You get to see her every day of the week. I only get to see you five days out of seven. Sometimes six."

Mary-Kate laughed. *What could be better,* she thought, *than having your secret admirer turn out to be your best friend?*

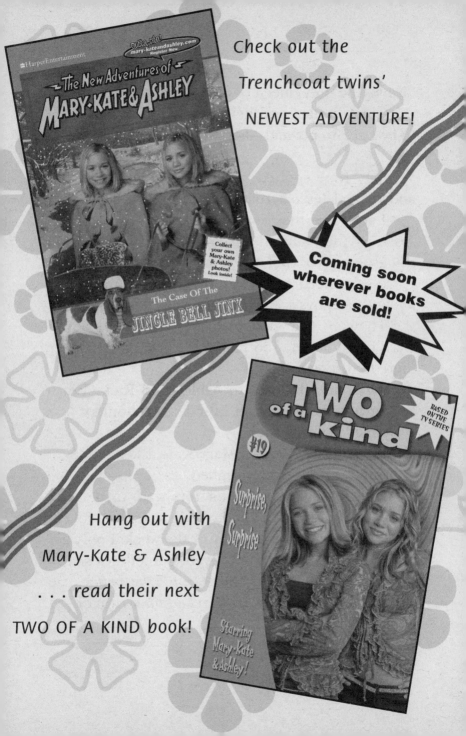

BE A CHARACTER IN A MARY-KATE & ASHLEY BOOK SWEEPSTAKES!

IT COULD BE YOU!

COMPLETE THIS ENTRY FORM:

ENTER

mary-kateandashley.com
America Online Keyword: mary-kateandashley

BE A CHARACTER IN A MARY-KATE & ASHLEY BOOK
Sweepstakes!

No purchase necessary. See details on back.

Name: _____

Address: _____

City: _____ State: _____ Zip: _____

Phone: _____ Age: _____

Mail to: **BE A CHARACTER IN A MARY-KATE
& ASHLEY BOOK SWEEPSTAKES!**
C/O HarperCollins Publishers
Attention: Children's Marketing Department
10 East 53rd Street
New York, NY 10022

HarperEntertainment
A Division of HarperCollins*Publishers*
www.harpercollins.com

TM & © 2001 Dualstar Entertainment Group, Inc.,
All logos character names, and other likenesses thereof
are the trademarks of Dualstar Entertainment Group, Inc.
All rights reserved. THE NEW ADVENTURES OF
MARY-KATE & ASHLEY TM & © 2001 Warner Bros., Inc.

PARACHUTE

DUALSTAR
PUBLICATIONS

THE NEW ADVENTURES OF MARY-KATE & ASHLEY™
Be a Character in a Mary-Kate & Ashley Book Sweepstakes

OFFICIAL RULES:

1. No purchase necessary.

2. To enter complete the official entry form or hand print your name, address, age, and phone number along with the words "THE NEW ADVENTURES OF MARY-KATE & ASHLEY™ Be a Character in a Mary-Kate & Ashley Book Sweepstakes" on a 3" x 5" card and mail to THE NEW ADVENTURES OF MARY-KATE & ASHLEY Be a Character in a Mary-Kate & Ashley Book Sweepstakes, c/o HarperEntertainment, Attn: Children's Marketing Department, 10 East 53rd Street, New York, NY 10022, postmarked **no later than January 31, 2002**. Enter as often as you wish, but each entry must be mailed separately. One entry per envelope. Partially completed, illegible, or mechanically reproduced entries will not be accepted. Sponsor, as defined below, is not responsible for lost, late, mutilated, illegible, stolen, postage due, incomplete, or misdirected entries. All entries become the property of Dualstar Entertainment Group, Inc., and will not be returned.

3. Sweepstakes open to all legal residents of the United States (excluding Rhode Island), who are between the ages of five and fifteen by January 31, 2002, excluding employees and immediate family members of HarperCollins Publishers Inc. ("HarperCollins"), Parachute Properties and Parachute Press, Inc., and their respective subsidiaries and affiliates, officers, directors, shareholders, employees, agents, attorneys, and other representatives (individually and collectively "Parachute"), Dualstar Entertainment Group, Inc., and its subsidiaries and affiliates, officers, directors, shareholders, employees, agents, attorneys, and other representatives (individually and collectively "Dualstar"), and their respective parent companies, affiliates, subsidiaries, advertising, promotion and fulfillment agencies, and the persons with whom each of the above are domiciled. Offer void where prohibited or restricted by law.

4. Odds of winning depend on the total number of entries received. All prizes will be awarded. Winners will be randomly drawn on or about February 15, 2002, by HarperEntertainment, whose decisions are final. Potential winners will be notified by mail and will be required to sign and return an affidavit of eligibility and release of liability within 14 days of notification. Prizes won by minors will be awarded to parent or legal guardian who must sign and return all required legal documents. By acceptance of their prize, winners consent to the use of their names, photographs, likenesses, and personal information by HarperCollins, Parachute, Dualstar, and for publicity purposes without further compensation except where prohibited.

5.a) One (1) Grand Prize winner will have his or her name included in a Mary-Kate & Ashley book, as a character; and receive an autographed copy of the book in which the winner's name appears. HarperCollins, Parachute, and Dualstar reserve the right to substitute another prize of equal or greater value in the event that the winner is unable to receive the prize for any reason. Approximate retail value: $4.25.

b) Fifty (50) First Prize winners win an autographed Mary-Kate & Ashley book. Approximate total retail value: $212.50.

6. Only one prize will be awarded per individual, family, or household. Prizes are non-transferable and cannot be sold or redeemed for cash. No cash substitute is available. Any federal, state, or local taxes are the responsibility of the winner. Sponsor may substitute prize of equal or greater value, if necessary, due to availability.

7. Additional terms: By participating, entrants agree a) to the official rules and decisions of the judges, which will be final in all respects; and to waive any claim to ambiguity of the official rules and b) to release, discharge, and hold harmless HarperCollins, Parachute, Dualstar, and their affiliates, subsidiaries, and advertising and promotion agencies from and against any and all liability or damages associated with acceptance, use, or misuse of any prize received in this sweepstakes.

8. Any dispute arising from this Sweepstakes will be determined according to the laws of the State of New York, without reference to its conflict of law principles, and the entrants consent to the personal jurisdiction of the State and Federal courts located in New York County and agree that such courts have exclusive jurisdiction over all such disputes.

9. To obtain the name of the winners, please send your request and a self-addressed stamped envelope (excluding residents of Vermont and Washington) to:

   THE NEW ADVENTURES OF MARY-KATE & ASHLEY™ Be a Character in a Mary-Kate & Ashley Book Sweepstakes
   c/o HarperEntertainment
   10 East 53rd Street, New York, NY 10022
   by March 1, 2002. Sweepstakes sponsor: HarperCollins Publishers, Inc.

Jet to London
with Mary-Kate and Ashley!

All-new movie!

Own it on video today!

The Ultimate Fan's

mary-kate

Don't miss

The New Adventures of MARY-KATE & ASHLEY™

- ❏ The Case Of The Great Elephant Escape
- ❏ The Case Of The Summer Camp Caper
- ❏ The Case Of The Surfing Secret
- ❏ The Case Of The Green Ghost
- ❏ The Case Of The Big Scare Mountain Mystery
- ❏ The Case Of The Slam Dunk Mystery
- ❏ The Case Of The Rock Star's Secret
- ❏ The Case Of The Cheerleading Camp Mystery

- ❏ The Case Of The Flying Phantom
- ❏ The Case Of The Creepy Castle
- ❏ The Case Of The Golden Slipper
- ❏ The Case Of The Flapper 'Napper
- ❏ The Case Of The High Seas Secret
- ❏ The Case Of The Logical I Ranch
- ❏ The Case Of The Dog Camp Mystery
- ❏ The Case Of The Screaming Scarecrow

Starring in

- ❏ Switching Goals
- ❏ Our Lips Are Sealed
- ❏ Winning London
- ❏ School Dance Party

📚 **HarperEntertainment**
An Imprint of HarperCollinsPublishers
www.harpercollins.com

mary-kateandashley.com
America Online Keyword: mary-kateandashley

DUALSTAR
PUBLICATIONS

PARACHUTE

Books created and produced by Parachute Publishing, L.L.C., in cooperation with Dualstar Publications, a division of Dualstar Entertainment Group, Inc.
TWO OF A KIND TM & © 2001 Warner Bros. THE NEW ADVENTURES OF MARY-KATE & ASHLEY and STARRING IN TM & © 2001 Dualstar Entertainment Group, Inc.

Reading Checklist

andashley

single one!

MAKE YOUR OWN MOVIE MAGIC™
WITH THE
MARY-KATE AND ASHLEY
CELEBRITY PREMIERE FASHION DOLLS

AVAILABLE
MARCH 2001

Go behind the scenes a
Mary-Kate gets ready...

...and Ashley sets
the scene.

mary-kateandashley.com
America Online Keyword: mary-kateandashley

DUALSTAR
CONSUMER PRODUCTS

mary~kateandashley

GAME GIRLS
mary-kateandashley
VIDEO GAMES

Join in on the Fun!

Real Games for Real Girls™

Available NOW!